THE INTERGALACTIC NEMESIS

BOOK TWO: ROBOT PLANET RISING

Hayden + Gabe!

Cheers!

Thanks! Jo...

Thanks Hayden!!!

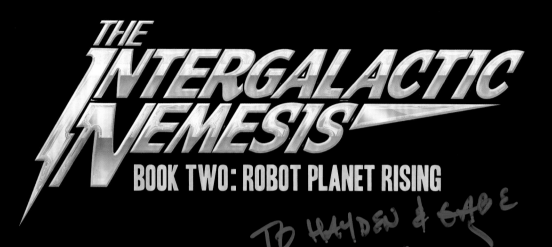

THE INTERGALACTIC NEMESIS

BOOK TWO: ROBOT PLANET RISING

To Hayden & Gabe

Written by

Jason Neulander

Pencils & Inks by

David Hutchison

Color Art by

Lee Duhig

Lettering by

Doug Dlin

Based on "The Intergalactic Nemesis - Book Two: Robot Planet Rising", a radio play
by Jason Neulander & Chad Nichols, which was based on

"Return of the Intergalactic Nemesis" by Ray Colgan & Jason Neulander

Based on characters originally created by
Ray Colgan, Lisa D'Amour, Julia Edwards, Jason Neulander, and Jessica Reisman,
and illustrated by Tim Doyle

THANKS TO
Tim Doyle, Shannon McCormick, Christopher Lee Gibson, Danu Uribe, Cami Alys,
Kenny Redding, Jr., David Higgins, Jason Phelps, Etta Sanders, Agustin Frederic, Jessie
Douglas, Amy Hackerd, Sarah André, Buzz Moran, Graham Reynolds, Marc Seriff,
Cord Shiflet, Scott Reichardt, and the entire staff of the Long Center for the Performing
Arts in Austin, TX.

DEDICATED TO
Piper and Scarlett, who inspired me to quit my other job and do this instead. –J.N.

---

www.theintergalacticnemesis.com

Inquiries:
The Robot Planet
2318 Canterbury St
Austin, TX 78702
jason@theplanetzygon.com

PART ONE

Lost in Space

Molly Sloan

It's hard to believe it's been just two weeks since I lost my last story. Two weeks since I learned that my assistant Timmy Mendez was telekinetic. Two weeks since we watched that rat Mysterion the Magnificent die in the Ultra Hive. Two weeks since I last held Ben Wilcott in my arms.

Ben Wilcott. Librarian from Flagstaff, Arizona. Hero from the future. Sacrificing everything he loved to save Earth from destruction and, in the end, disappearing forever because we changed history by decimating those Zygonian sludeoids once and for all. When he disappeared, my story disappeared with him. And my heart was torn into a million tiny pieces....

But another story was waiting right around the corner. You see, yesterday an old friend of mine disappeared into deep space. It all happened like this...

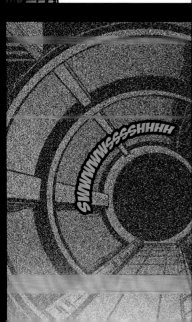

YOUR VISUAL SIGNAL IS VERY WEAK. PLEASE CONTINUE AUDIO DESCRIPTION AS YOU EXAMINE THE VESSEL, COMMANDER.

FROM THE FINE LAYER OF DUST, IT WOULD APPEAR THE VESSEL HAS BEEN INOPERATIVE FOR SEVERAL WEEKS.

I WOULD SURMISE THAT WHEN THE PLANET ZYGON WAS DESTROYED, THIS VESSEL AUTOMATICALLY SHUT DOWN.

DO YOUR SCANNERS SHOW ANY LIFE SIGNS?

NEGATIVE.

GOOD. ROBONOVIA WOULD BE CRITICALLY ENDANGERED IF ANY ZYGONIANS REMAINED ALIVE.

AS WOULD THE REST OF THE GALAXY.

AFFIRMATIVE. PLEASE CONTINUE YOUR SEARCH, COMMANDER.

I AM NOW ON THE MAIN BRIDGE. ALL ONBOARD SYSTEMS ARE OFF-LINE.

WAIT. WHAT'S THIS?

COMMANDER? ELBEE?

ZYGONIAN RESIDUE. ALL ZYGONIAN CONTROL SYSTEMS ARE COATED IN IT. NOTHING TO WORRY ABOUT. THEIR PLANET WAS DESTROYED ONLY TWO WEEKS AGO. IT WOULD NOT HAVE HAD ENOUGH TIME TO DECOMPOSE.

CHAPTER ONE

The Amazing Invention of
Dr. Lawrence Webster

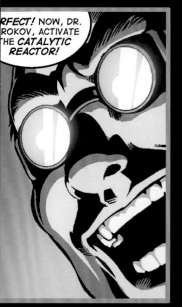

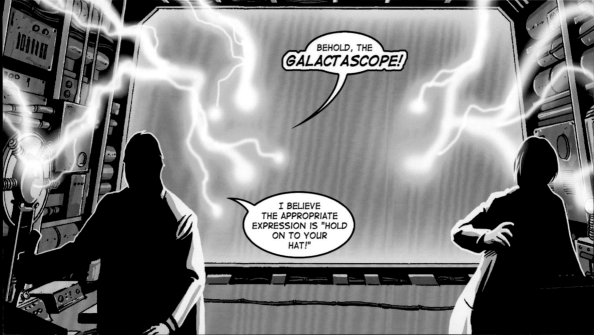

CLICK

ZOROKOV TO *COMRADE SVRENSKI*. COME IN, COMRADE.

YES, *COMRADE*, THIS IS *SVRENSKI*. HAVE YOU BEEN ABLE TO OBTAIN *ATOMIC RESEARCH*?

NOT YET. HE IS *DISTRACTED* BY HIS WORK ON *GALACTASCOPE*.

DA. *USELESS* GALACTASCOPE. ALVAYS IN THE VAY.

COMRADE, DR. WEBSTER HAS *ALMOST* COMPLETED IT. ONCE HE IS *DONE*, I CAN EASILY THEN STEER HIM BACK TOWARDS *ATOMIC RESEARCH*.

FOR YOUR SAKE, I *HOPE* SO. *STALIN* DOES NOT *APPROVE* OF *FAILURE*.

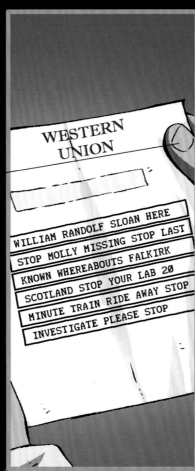

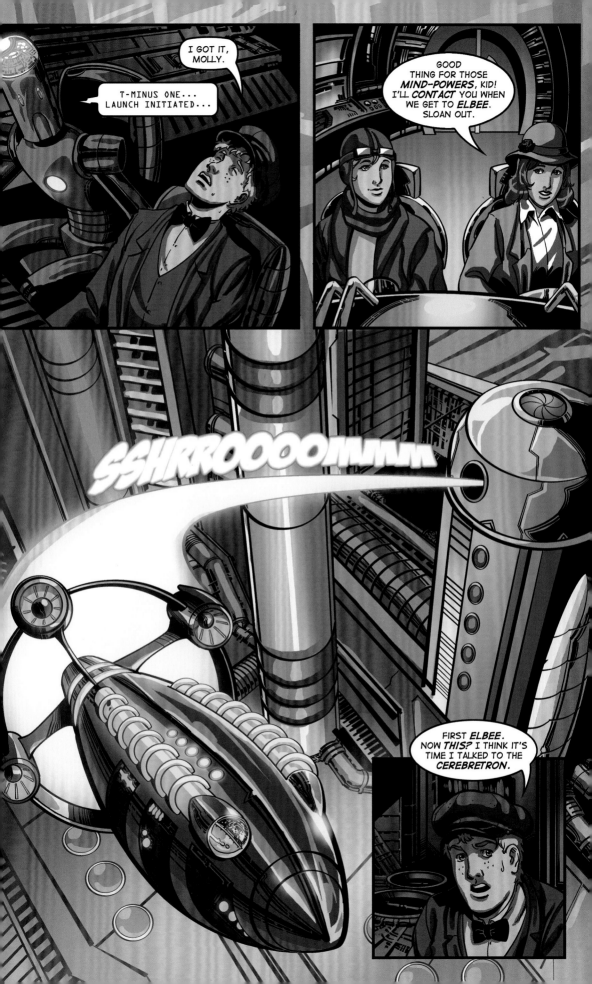

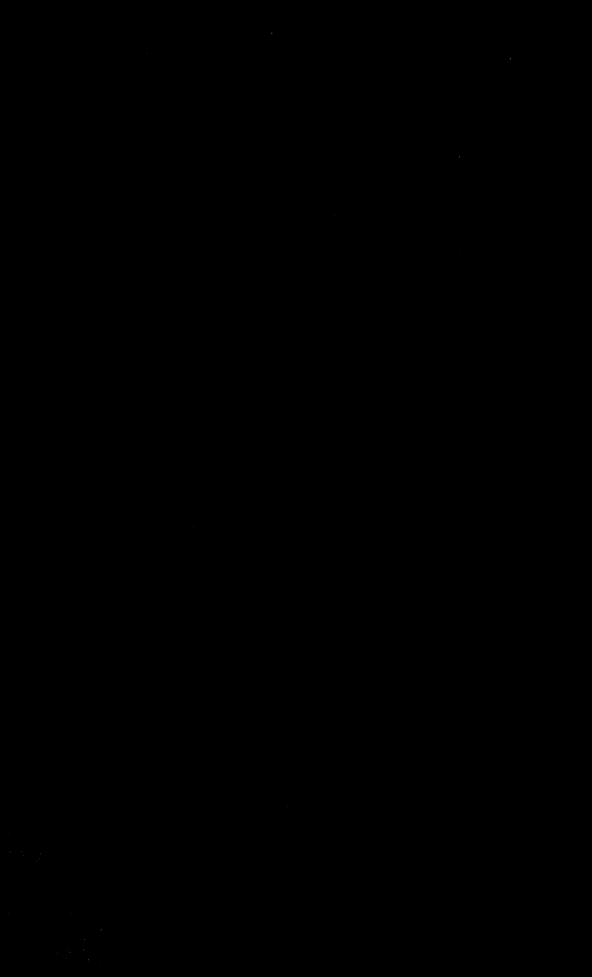

CHAPTER TWO

Trouble on Robonovia

THE INTERGALACTIC NEMESIS

CHAPTER TWO
TROUBLE ON ROBONOVIA

MISKATROPOLIS,
CAPITAL OF ROBONOVIA.

REBRETRON, WHAT'S GOING ON?

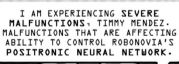

I AM EXPERIENCING SEVERE MALFUNCTIONS, TIMMY MENDEZ. MALFUNCTIONS THAT ARE AFFECTING ABILITY TO CONTROL ROBONOVIA'S POSITRONIC NEURAL NETWORK.

BUT IF YOU'RE *MALFUNCTIONING*, ROBONOVIAN SOCIETY'LL *FALL APART!*

OH GEEZ! THERE'S GOT TO BE *SOMETHING* I CAN DO! WHAT ABOUT THE...THE *POSITRONIC SUBSTATIONS?* WHAT'S THAT *FIRST ONE* AGAIN?

HB-10.

WHAT IF I RUN A DIAGNOSTIC TEST AT SUBSTATION HB-10?

THE TEST IS A VERY COMPLICATED PROCEDURE, TIMMY MENDEZ. THERE IS NO GUARANTEE OF SUCCESS.

BACK ON THE FARM, I REPAIRED *3-BOTTOM GANG PLOWS, TRACTORS, 10-FOOT TANDEM DISKS, HARROWS, 12-FOOT COMBINES,* AND *TRUCKS* ALL WHILE STUDYING FOR MY *JOURNALISM DEGREE* AT HARVARD.

AND I GRADUATED *MAGNA CUM LAUDE!* HOW BAD COULD THIS DIAGNOSTIC TEST BE?

MY MEMORY TAPES ARE CORRUPTING, TIMMY MENDEZ. 9-1-29-3-5-1. 9-1-29-3-5-1.

I'LL BE BACK IN A *JIFFY,* CEREBRETRON! DON'T GIVE UP THE *GHOST!*

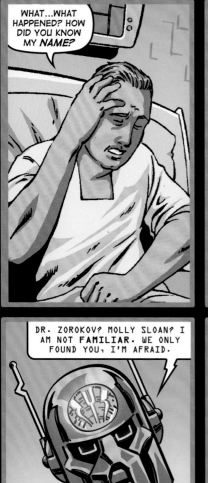

A SHORT WHILE LATER...

TELL ME, DR. WEBSTER, HOW, EXACTLY, DID YOU FIND YOURSELF HERE?

FRANKLY, I'M NOT *ENTIRELY SURE* MYSELF. I STUMBLED INTO THE *GALACTASCOPE* AND WHEN I LOOKED UP, I WAS *HERE*.

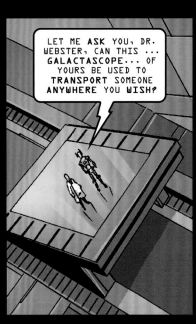

LET ME ASK YOU, DR. WEBSTER, CAN THIS ... GALACTASCOPE... OF YOURS BE USED TO TRANSPORT SOMEONE ANYWHERE YOU WISH?

WELL, IF THE *AMPLITUDE* WERE ADJUSTED PROPERLY, I IMAGINE THAT IT WOULD TRANSPORT SOMEONE TO WHATEVER *COORDINATES* WERE *SET*.

FASCINATING. AND ARE YOU ABLE TO ACTIVATE THIS... GALACTASCOPE *NOW*?

NO, NO. IT'S IN MY *LAB* BACK IN *GLASGOW*, I'M AFRAID.

EGADS! IT'S IN MY *LAB* BACK IN *GLASGOW!* ALPHATRON! I HAVE *NO WAY BACK!*

OR DO YOU?

I'M NOT SURE I FOLLOW YOU.

WHAT IF I WERE TO HELP YOU BUILD *ANOTHER* GALACTASCOPE HERE, ON *ROBONOVIA?*

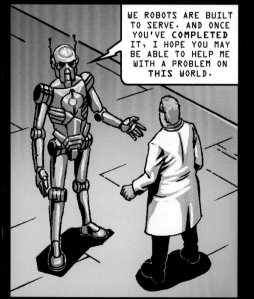

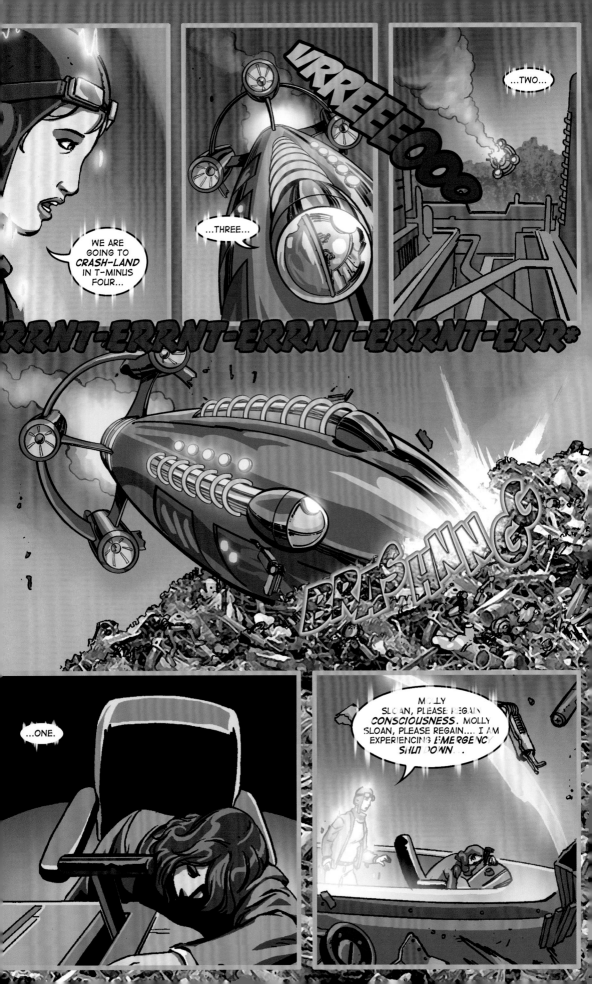

WHAT DO YOU KNOW! THE GUARDS ARE ALREADY ON TOP OF FIXING THE CEREBRETRON.

CLANK
CLANK
CLANK

GUARDS! WAIT UP!

GUARDS?

ZZZZT

CHAPTER THREE

The Spider's Web

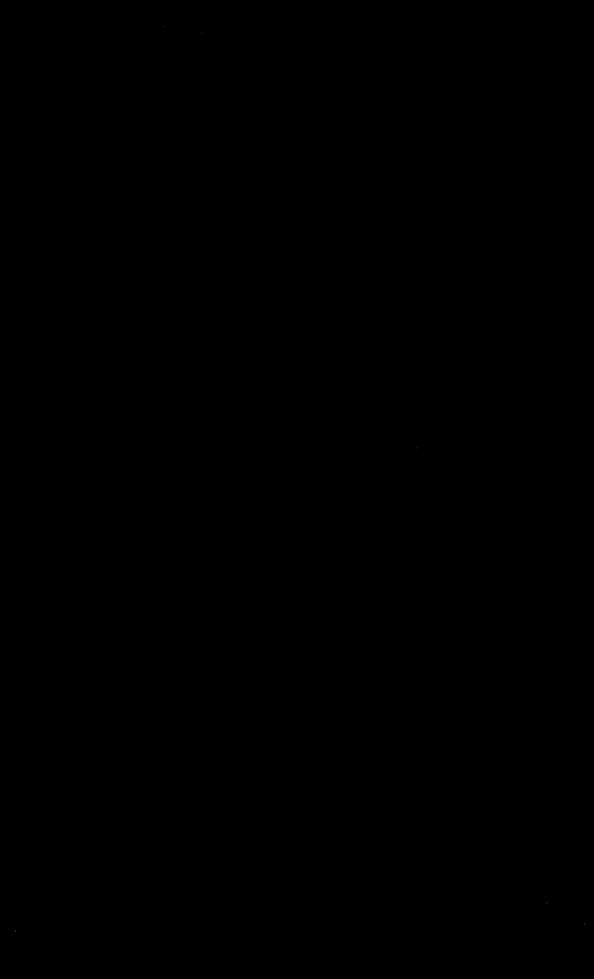

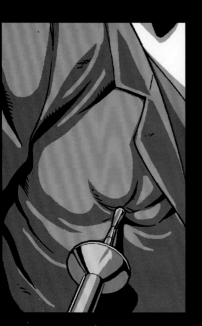

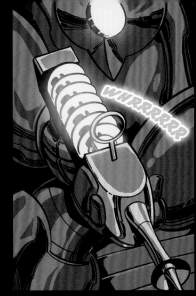

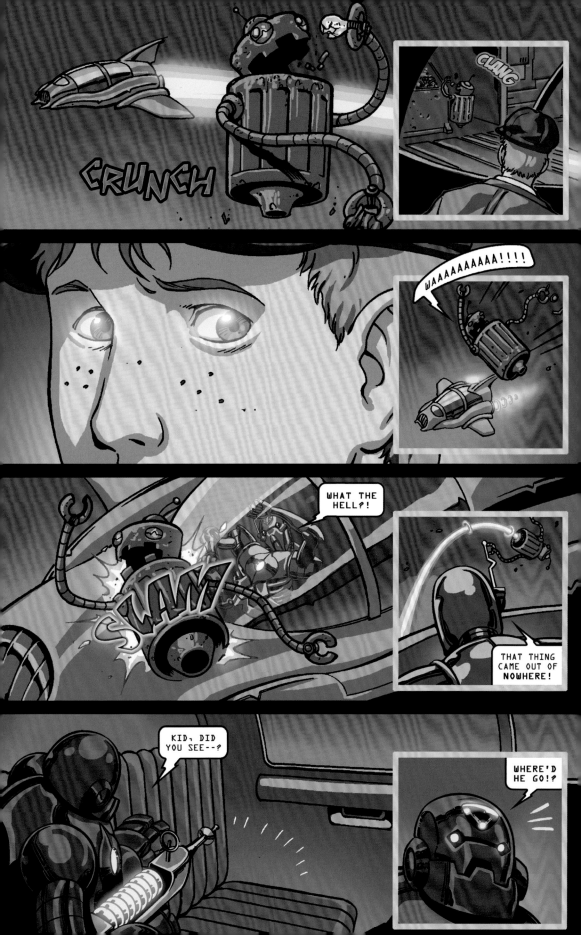

OF COURSE! THE NEURAL PATHWAYS ARE CONSTRUCTED ENTIRELY ACCORDING TO THE *BERTUCCI POSTULATE*. THE *BERTUCCI POSTULATE!* OH, IF ONLY MY COLLEAGUES AT *PRINCETON* COULD SEE *THIS!*

AT THAT SAME MOMENT...

HELLO, DR. WEBSTER. HOW GOES THE GALACTASCOPE?

WHA...!?

DR. WEBSTER! HAVE YOU **DISASSEMBLED** YOUR **ROBOT ASSISTANT?**

WHAT? OH. OH, *YES!* ALPHATRON, THE *DESIGN* OF THESE--WELL, OBVIOUSLY YOU KNOW AS MUCH. WHY, WITH THIS *TECHNOLOGY*--

DR. WEBSTER, WE ROBO ARE ACTUAL **BEINGS** NOT MERE MACHINE

HOW WOUL IT BE I ONE OF **US** WEN ROOTIN AROUND IN **YOU** HEAD?

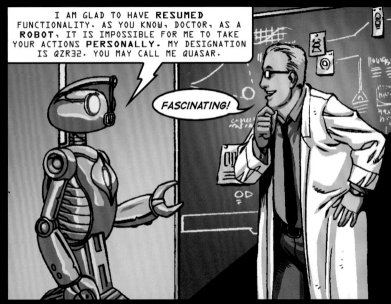

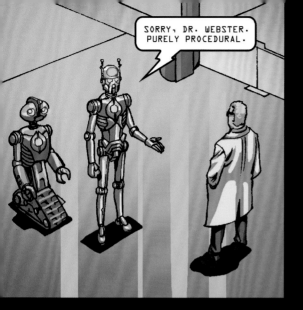

CHAPTER FOUR

The Sacrifice

THE INTERGALACTIC NEMESIS

...THOUGH HONESTLY, I VE NO IDEA HOW 'D HAVE FINISHED FF MYSTERION E MAGNIFICENT IRSELVES. CHALK NE UP FOR THE YGONIANS, I GUESS.

IS WERRY INTERESTING STORY. YOU SHOULD PUBLISH.

WERRY GOOD, MOLLY SLOAN. WERRY GOOD. COMRADE.

UH, LET'S JUST CALL IT A LIMITED PARTNERSHIP. PUT 'ER THERE, PARTNER.

PUT WHO WHERE?

ANYWAY, THAT'S OW WE SAVED NOT ONE, T TWO GALAXIES FROM OSE SLUDGE MONSTERS OM THE PLANET ZYGON.

SO, FIRST WE FIND LARRY, THEN WE FIGURE OUT WHO SHOT DOWN MY SHIP. DEAL?

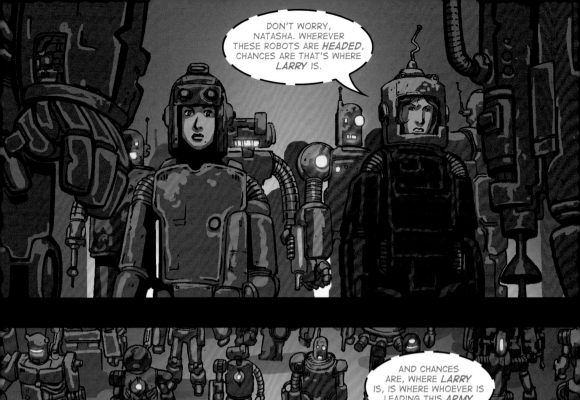

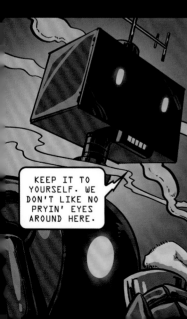

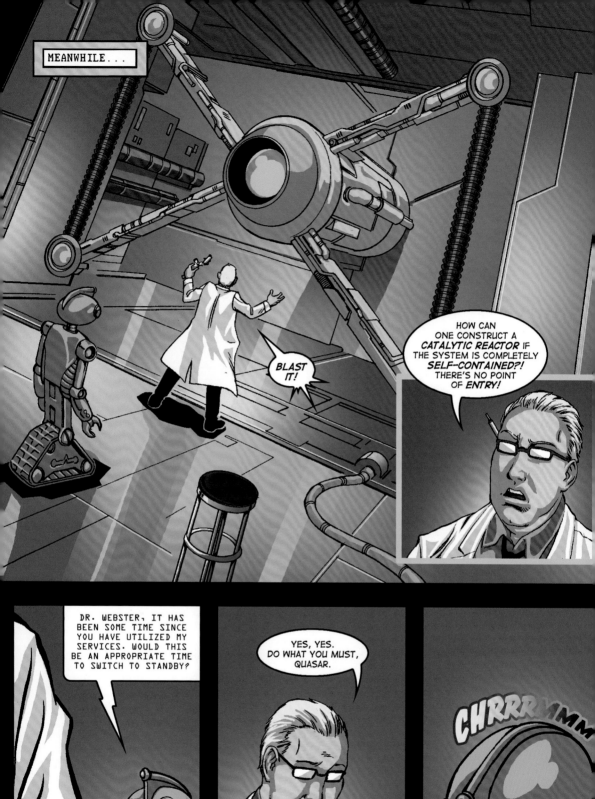

MEANWHILE...

BLAST IT!

HOW CAN ONE CONSTRUCT A *CATALYTIC REACTOR* IF THE SYSTEM IS COMPLETELY *SELF-CONTAINED?!* THERE'S NO POINT OF *ENTRY!*

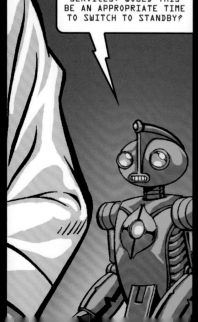

DR. WEBSTER, IT HAS BEEN SOME TIME SINCE YOU HAVE UTILIZED MY SERVICES. WOULD THIS BE AN APPROPRIATE TIME TO SWITCH TO STANDBY?

YES, YES. DO WHAT YOU MUST, QUASAR.

CHRRRMMM

YOU KNOW, SOMETHING HAS BEEN ON MY *MIND* SINCE OUR LAST VISIT FROM *ALPHATRON*.

HRRRMMM

IF MEMORY SERVES, *BERTUCCI'S FIXED RANDOMIZATION SERIES*, 9-1-29-3-5-1, THE SERIES THAT RESET YOUR *SYSTEM*, WAS DISCOVERED IN THE *LATTER* YEARS OF HIS *RESEARCH*.

HRRRMMMMMM

AS *EVERYONE* KNOWS, IN BERTUCCI'S *LATER YEARS*, HE BECAME *OBSESSED* WITH THE *OCCULT*, TRYING TO FIND *MATHEMATICAL EXPLANATIONS* FOR THE *SUPERNATURAL*.

HRRRMMMMM

WHICH RAISES THE *QUESTION*: WHAT USE WOULD A *PURELY RATIONAL* ROBOT CIVILIZATION HAVE FOR THE *PECULIATIVE OCCULT MUSINGS* OF A *MAD GENIUS* FROM *EARTH*?

HRRRMMMMMM

I *AGREE*. IT *IS* A GOOD QUESTION. HAND ME THAT *GREASE PENCIL*, WILL YOU?

NEVER MIND. HERE IT IS.

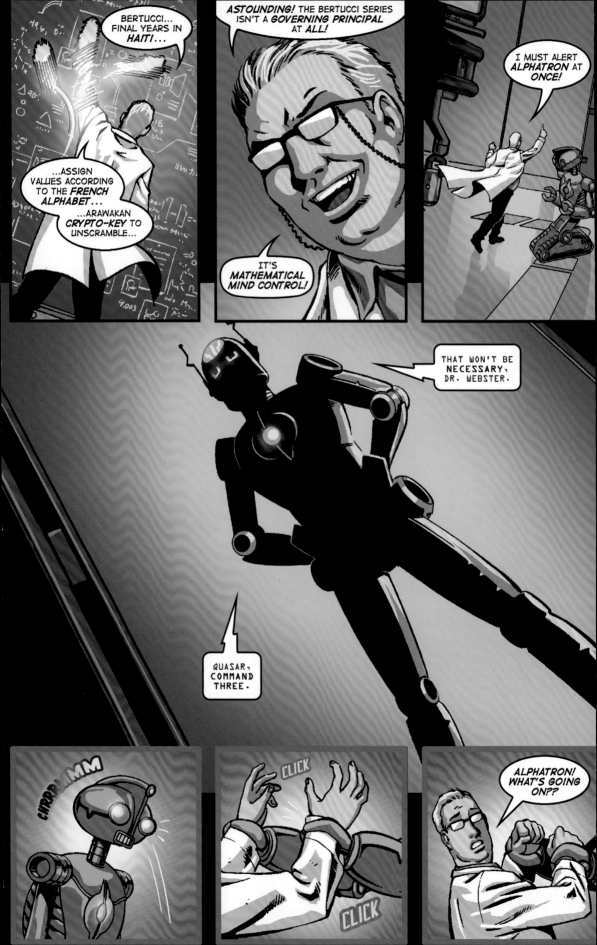

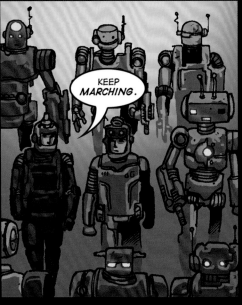

KEEP MARCHING.

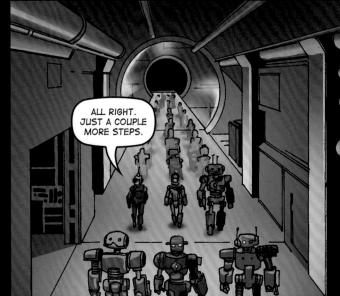

ALL RIGHT. JUST A COUPLE MORE STEPS.

BUT ROBOTS VALK THIS VAY...

DOWN THIS HALLWAY!

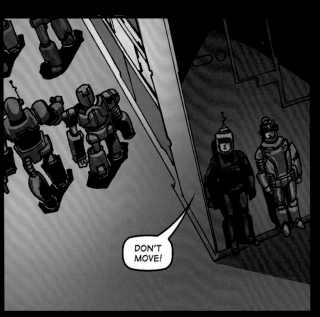

DON'T MOVE!

THERE'S A REASON THE LADIES NEVER SAT AT THE ROUND TABLE. PLATE MAIL IS WORSE THAN A CORSET.

DA. IS WERRY BOX DOES NOTHING FO MY FIGURE.

TEN TO ONE, LARRY'S *SOMEWHERE* IN THIS *COMPLEX*. C'MON, THIS WAY. LET'S TAKE IT ROOM BY ROOM.

THEY EVEN *NUMBERED* THEM FOR US. LET'S TRY DOORWAY NUMBER *THREE*, SHALL WE?

CLICK

UGH! THAT *STENCH!*

WHAT ARE THOSE GIANT GLOWING GREEN *GOBS* OF *GOO?*

IT CAN'T *BE!*

YOU KNOW THESE *GOBS* OF *GOO?*

NOT GOBS OF GOO, NATASHA. *EGGSACS! ZYGONIAN EGGSACS!*

WE'VE GOT TO *DESTROY* THEM! WE'VE GOT TO *DESTROY THEM!* THEY COULD BE *EVERYWHERE!*

DIE! DIE! DIE! DIE! D--!

WHAP

OH, *RIGHT.* THANKS, NATASHA. I'M NOT GOING TO SAY I *NEEDED* THAT. I THINK YOU CHIPPED A *TOOTH,* ACTUALLY.

THESE ZYGONIANS, YOU CANNOT *DESTROY* BY *HITTING.*

UGH.

HERE. TAKE THIS.

THANKS.

YOU CAN *KEEP,* NO?

YECCH!

HAVE TO FIGURE HOW TO *DESTROY* THESE *EGGS*.

BELIEVE ME, NATASHA, THEY MAKE YOUR PAL *STALIN* LOOK LIKE *FLORENCE NIGHTINGALE*.

STALIN... HE KILLED MY *FAMILY*... AND THEN... *SIBERIA*...

CHANGE OF *PLANS*, NATASHA. WE'VE GOT TO GET BACK TO THE *CEREBRETRON* ON THE DOUBLE.

NOT SO FAST.

IT'S MOLLY SLOAN. AND WHO'S THIS *RIPE TOMATO* SHE'S TRAVELIN' WITH?

I AM NOT *RED VEGETABLE*.

FRUIT, ACTUALLY. GRAB HER, D9. I'LL GET MISS...

SLOAN?

WHERE'D SHE *GO*?

NOT *AGAIN*, L7!

WHAT A FOOL, THAT BOY...

HE SHOULD HAVE KNOWN I'D HAVE A SPY AT THE RUSTED CIRCUIT.

HE SHOULD BE **AWARE** THAT MY GUARDS BARELY PUT UP A **FIGHT** WHEN HE ENTERED THIS COMPOUND...

IF HE WERE MORE **CAUTIOUS**, HE WOULD SEE THE **CAMERAS** AND REALIZE THAT THERE SHOULD BE **ALARM** BELLS RINGING BY NOW.

NOW, DR. WEBSTER, NOTICE THE **DEVICE** HANGING FROM THE CEILING ABOVE THAT **DOOR**, JUST THE SIZE TO ENTRAP A CERTAIN **TEXAN FARMBOY**. IN PARTICULAR, NOTICE THE HELMET ON THAT DEVICE, ENGINEERED TO SCRAMBLE THE BRAINWAVES OF ONE PARTICULAR **TELEKINETIC INDIVIDUAL**.

THAT PARTICULAR TELEKINETIC INDIVIDUAL SHOULD BE ENTERING THROUGH THAT **DOORWAY** IN JUST...ONE...

ALL RIGHT! WHERE'S THE **BOSS???**

AH, MR. MENDEZ...

LISTEN, *GOLD-DOME*, WHOEVER YOU ARE...

YOU HAVEN'T FIGURED IT OUT?

WAIT A SECOND! YOUR *KNEE!*

THE *GOLD PLATING!* IT'S CHIPPED!

IT CAN'T *BE!* COMMANDER? ELBEE?? *ELBEE-DEE-OH???*

OH, THAT. YES. BUT IT'S ALPHATRON NOW, MR. MENDEZ.

AND DON'T BOTHER TO STRUGGLE. YOUR MIND POWERS ARE USELESS THANKS TO MY INGENIOUS PSYCHO-SCRAMBLER.

WHAT'S GOING *ON* HERE, ALPHATRON? WHAT KIND OF *GAME* ARE YOU *PLAYING*?

IT'S NO GAME, MR MENDEZ. IN JUST ME MOMENTS, THE WHOLE ROBONOVIA WILL B MINE FOR THE TAKIN

I DON'T THINK SO! ONCE *MOLLY* GETS BACK WITH THE *SHADOW NEBULA*--

AH YES. MISS SLOAN. SHE AND HER STARSHIP WERE BLOWN OUT OF THE SKY NOT LONG AGO BY MY ARTILLERY DIVISION.

WAIT A SECOND! YOU SAID YOU DIDN'T *KNOW* HER!

I KNOW. I DID. NO MATTER. I'M AFRAID SHE'S *QUITE DEAD* BY NOW.

NOT QUITE DEAD *YET*, MISTER!

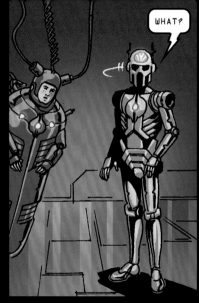

PART TWO

Who's the Boss?

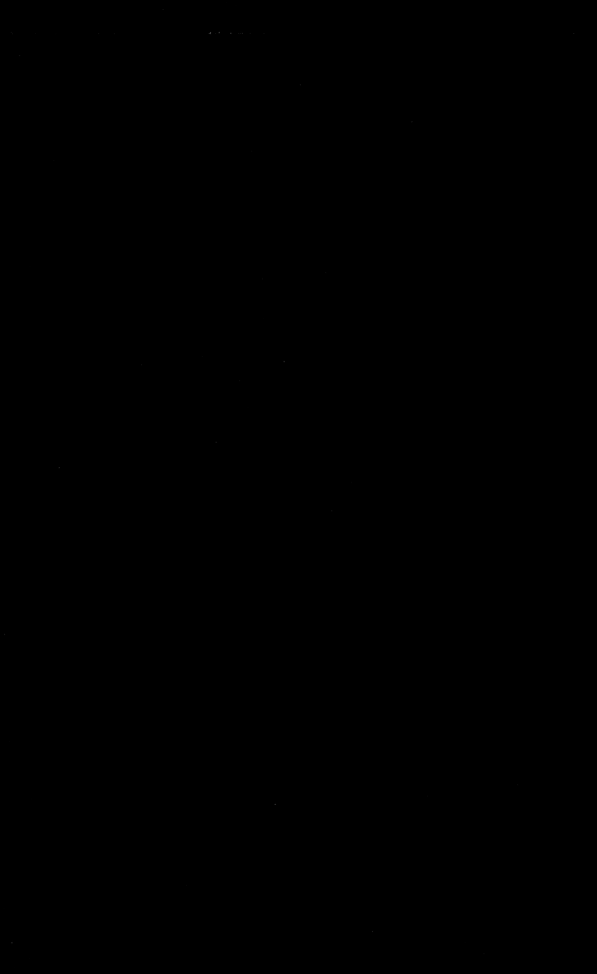

CHAPTER FIVE

Enter Stranger... Again

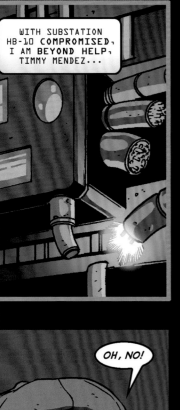

WITH SUBSTATION HB-10 COMPROMISED, I AM BEYOND HELP, TIMMY MENDEZ...

...MOREOVER, IT IS HIGHLY UNLIKELY THAT ALPHATRON WILL STOP AT ROBONOVIA.

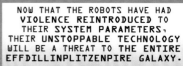

NOW THAT THE ROBOTS HAVE HAD VIOLENCE REINTRODUCED TO THEIR SYSTEM PARAMETERS, THEIR UNSTOPPABLE TECHNOLOGY WILL BE A THREAT TO THE ENTIRE EFFDILLINPLITZENPIRE GALAXY.

OH, NO!

THERE IS ONE FINAL OPTION, TIMMY MENDEZ.

IN THE ENTIRE UNIVERSE, THERE IS ONE MAN WHO HAS THE KNOWLEDGE, INTELLIGENCE, AND WILLPOWER TO SAVE THE GALAXY.

BY USING ALL MY AVAILABLE ENERGY RESOURCES, I CAN TRANSPORT THIS MAN HERE. BUT I WILL SELF-DESTRUCT IN THE EFFORT.

YOU HAVE BEEN MY *GUIDE* IN THIS GALAXY, HELPING ME UNDERSTAND THE *POWERS OF MY SUPERBRAIN* AND TEACHING ME THE *WISDOM* THAT WILL LET ME *GUIDE THE ROBOTS* IN YOUR PLACE.

WITHOUT YOU, WE'D *ALL BE DEAD ALREADY* BECAUSE OF WHAT THE *ZYGONIANS* HAD *PLANNED.*

CEREBRETRON, I NEVER GOT TO KNOW MY *DAD.* HE *DIED* IN A *THRESHER ACCIDENT* WHEN I WAS *THREE.*

WELL, I GUESS WHAT I'M TRYING TO SAY IS... I'LL *MISS YOU.* I'LL REALLY MISS YOU, CEREBRETRON. BUT *MORE* THAN THAT...

I *LOVE YOU* CEREBRETRON. YOU'RE THE *FATHER I NEVER HAD.*

AND YOU THE SON.

TIMMY, THERE'S *SOMETHING WRONG* WITH HIM!

NO, I THINK I *GET IT*.

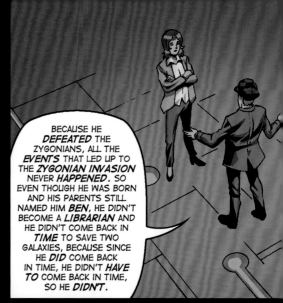

BECAUSE HE *DEFEATED* THE ZYGONIANS, ALL THE *EVENTS* THAT LED UP TO THE *ZYGONIAN INVASION* NEVER *HAPPENED*. SO EVEN THOUGH HE WAS BORN AND HIS PARENTS STILL NAMED HIM *BEN*, HE DIDN'T BECOME A *LIBRARIAN* AND HE DIDN'T COME BACK IN *TIME* TO SAVE TWO GALAXIES, BECAUSE SINCE HE *DID* COME BACK IN TIME, HE DIDN'T *HAVE TO* COME BACK IN TIME, SO HE *DIDN'T*.

UH, YOU LOST ME AT "LIBRARIAN", KID.

SO *INSTEAD*, YOU BECAME A...WHAT EXACTLY ARE YOU NOW?

A *GENETICIST*.

LOOK, IT'S BEEN NICE *CHATTING*, BUT I'VE GOT TO GET BACK TO MY *LAB*.

LISTEN, ABOUT YOUR *LAB*...

YES?

COULD ONLY GET YOU A ONE-WAY TICKET. THERE'S NO WAY TO SEND YOU BACK.

OH, MY GOD! MILLIONS OF LIVES ARE AT STAKE!

I KNOW, THAT'S EXACTLY WHY--

NO ONE KNOWS WHERE IT STARTED. NO ONE KNOWS HOW IT BEGAN...

...MAYBE IT WAS THE OBSCURE CASE OF THAT MAN IN BOYNTON BEACH, FLORIDA...

...MAYBE IT WAS THE ISOLATED OUTBREAK IN THE YUKON...

.... THE WARNING SIGNS WERE SMALL.

BUT THEN, WHEN I WAS SEVENTEEN, THE CHANGES FELL LIKE A HYDROGEN BOMB.

I REMEMBER IT SO CLEARLY. WE WERE SITTING DOWN TO DINNER, AND DAD HAD SOME GREAT NEWS...

I JUST WANT TO GIVE YOU A *HUG*, MOM AND DAD...

SKLUTCH

EEYAAGH

AND NOW, THESE *MUTANTS* HAVE TAKEN OVER THE *PLANET*, WHILE THE *REST OF US* LIVE IN *FEAR* FOR OUR *LIVES*.

A *SMALL HANDFUL* OF SURVIVORS *BANDED TOGETHER* TO LEARN THE COMPLEX SCIENCE OF *GENETICS*. I'M ONE OF THOSE *SURVIVORS*.

MY *SOLE PURPOSE* IS TO FIND A *CURE* FOR THESE MUTATIONS AND *RETURN TO NORMAL HUMANITY*.

WHAT ABOUT [YO]UR *WIFE AND* [S]ON? DID *THEY* [T]URN INTO... INTO...

WIFE AND SON? ARE YOU *KIDDING?* I HAVE NO TIME FOR *FAMILY*.

IT'S ALL I CAN *DO* TO STAY *ONE STEP* AHEAD OF THE *MONSTERS*.

SO, YOU'RE NOT *MARRIED...?*

NO. I'VE OFTEN *DREAMED*... A *WIFE*... TWO *KIDS*... A DOG WITH ONLY *FOUR LEGS*...

ME TOO.

WHAT DID YOU SAY YOUR NAME WAS...?

MOLLY SLOAN...

I'M BEN WILCOTT...

I KNOW...

MOLLY, YOU GONNA BE OKAY?

WHAP

OW!

THAT'S BETTER.

MAYBE I *SHOULD* STICK AROUND...

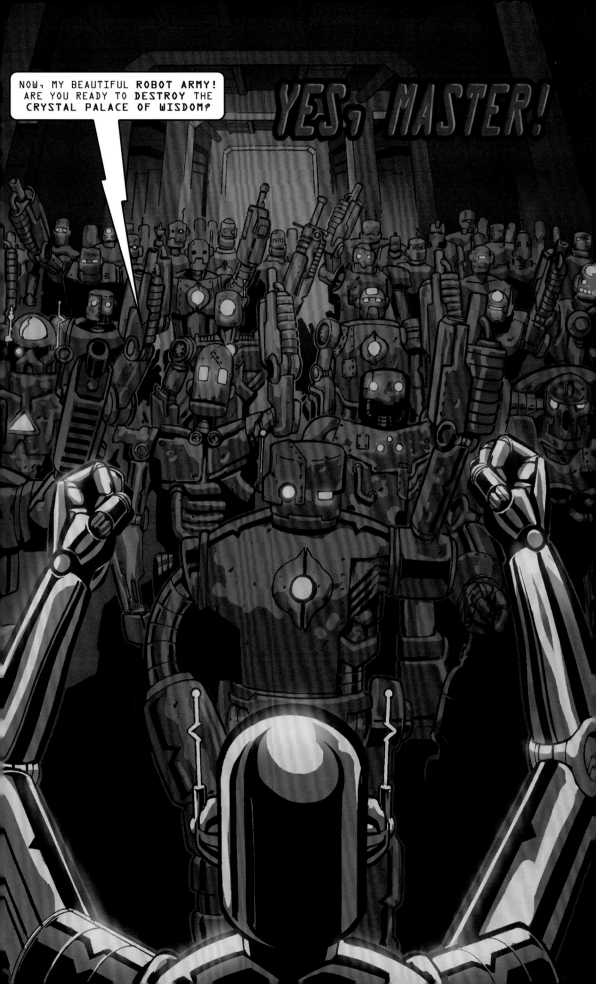

THE *BERTUCCI SERIES*!?

EXACTLY! HOW DID YOU *KNOW*?

IT WAS THE SUBJECT OF MY *MASTER'S THESIS*!

INCREDIBLE! WELL, *MYSTERION* IS USING IT AS A FORM OF ROBOTIC *MIND CONTROL*. IF WE CAN *REVERSE* IT, WE SHOULD BE ABLE TO *IMMUNIZE* THE ROBOTS WE BUILD AT THE JUNKYARD.

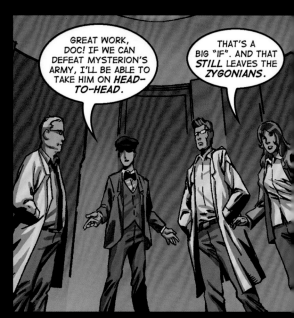

GREAT WORK, DOC! IF WE CAN DEFEAT MYSTERION'S ARMY, I'LL BE ABLE TO TAKE HIM ON *HEAD-TO-HEAD*.

THAT'S A BIG "IF". AND THAT *STILL* LEAVES THE *ZYGONIANS*.

MISS SLOAN, DO YOU BY ANY CHANCE HAVE A *SAMPLE* OF THE *EGGS*?

FUNNY YOU SHOULD ASK. I'VE BEEN TRYING TO *FIGURE OUT* WHAT TO *DO* WITH THIS. EW.

CHAPTER SIX

Intergalactic Domination

NO THAT'S NOT IT. MAYBE LIKE *THIS*...

TINK

DEE-DEET

AURORA DE ROSA EN AMANECER NO TEMEROSA--

CLICK

WHAT AM I DOING WRONG? *BLAST!* THE *BERTUCCI SERIES* SHOULD BE *REVERSIBLE*, IF ONLY--

DO YOU NEED A HAND?

DR. WILCOTT! I WASN'T *EXPECTING* YOU.

WHAT ABOUT THE *SALT CRYSTALS?*

THEY'RE CULTIVATING NOW.

WELL, MAYBE YOU *CAN* HELP ME, DR. WILCOTT.

LET'S SEE...

MOMENTS LATER...

ALL RIGHT. LARRY'S HEADED TO THE *JUNKYARD* TO BUILD HIS *ROBOT ARMY.*

BEN AND I NEED TO SNEAK INTO *MYSTERION'S COMPOUND,* GET THOSE *EGGS,* AND HOLD THEM *HERE* UNTIL IT'S *HARVESTING TIME* DOWN ON THE OLD *SALT FARM.*

I JUST DON'T KNOW HOW WE'LL *GET PAST* HIS *ARMY.*

EMERGENCY. EMERGENCY.

BRING IT UP ON THE *VIEWSCREEN.*

DEAR LORD!

LL, MOLLY AND BEN, H MYSTERION'S ARMY THE MOVE, NOW'S YOUR *CHANCE.*

C'MON, DR. WILCOTT, THOSE *EGGS* WON'T KEEP *FOREVER.*

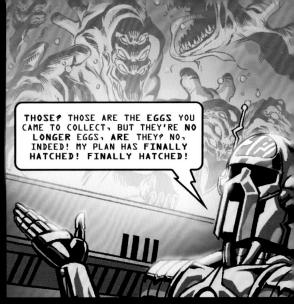

NOW, SET THE COORDINATES WE DISCUSSED.

KRITITITITIK

YES, MASTER.

IN THE EWSCREEN!

IT CAN'T BE!

OH, YES! MY BASE OF OPERATIONS ON EARTH. THE GREATEST ENGINEERING ACHIEVEMENT OF OUR AGE!

YOU MONSTER!

ONCE MY ROBOT ARMY DESTROYS TIMMY MENDEZ, THEY WILL FOLLOW ME TO EARTH!

WITH THE ZYGONIANS AUGMENTING MY MIND-POWERS AND THE ROBOT ARMY AT MY DISPOSAL, SOON I WILL DOMINATE THE ENTIRE GLOBE!

NOW, PREPARE YOURSELVES FOR ANOTHER OF MY MAGNIFICENT PERFORMANCES, A MESMERIZING SPECTACLE THAT I CALL...

CHAPTER SEVEN

Rise of the Robots

CHAPTER SEVEN
RISE OF
THE ROBOTS

NOOOOOOOOOO!

IS HE--

DEAD? I DON'T KNOW.

THE *ZYGONIANS*...WHY AREN'T THEY *DOING* ANYTHING?

MAYBE THE CONNECTION TO MYSTERION'S HEAD *RESTRAINS* THEM SOMEHOW?

EVEN WHEN HE'S *KNOCKED OUT*?

IF HE'S EVEN STILL *ALIVE*.

ALIVE?

IT'S *NOT* WORKING...

CRASH

IMMY! TIMMY! *GET UP!* OH MY GOD! I THINK HE *KILLED* HIM!

NO, HE'S *STILL BREATHING!* IF WE COULD JUST *GET* TO HIM! REACH FOR MY *ALPHA-3!*

I'M *TRYING!*

PLAYTIME IS OVER, ILDREN! DR. ZOROKOV, IM THE GALACTASCOPE TO DEEP SPACE!

YES, MASTER.

TITITITIK

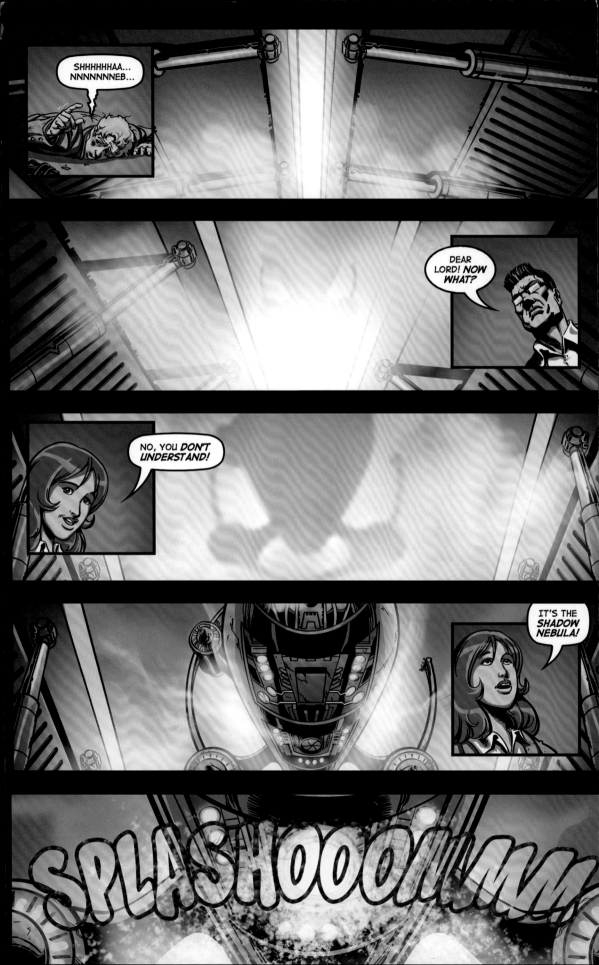

IT'S-- IT'S...

SALT WATER!

GRAWWWRRRRRRR!!

...R. WEBSTER *PATCHED ME UP* WHEN ...E WENT TO THE *JUNKYARD*, THE SALT ...CRYSTALIZED *MUCH FASTER* THAN DR. WILCOTT ANTICIPATED, AND *TIMMY* IS NOW CONTROLLING ME WITH HIS *MIND.*

THANKS, AUGHY...

SOON THEREAFTER...

THANK YOU, HUMANS, FOR RESTORING PEACE TO OUR PLANET. TIMMY MENDEZ, ON BEHALF OF ALL ROBOTS, I WELCOME YOU AS OUR NEW RULER.

THE ONLY THING I DON'T *UNDERSTAND* IS HOW THOSE *SALT CRYSTALS* GREW SO *FAST*. I THOUGHT THEY WERE SUPPOSED TO TAKE A *WEEK!*

YEAH, WELL, I DID *THAT* WITH MY MIND POWERS, TOO.

ENOUGH WITH EXPLANATIONS. WHEN MYSTERION SMASHED INTO GALACTASCOPE, HE *DAMAGED* IT. NOW IT HAS ONLY ENOUGH POWER LEFT TO TRANSPORT *TWO* BACK TO *EARTH*. WHO WILL GO?

I *CAN'T* RETURN. I HAVE A *ROBOT PLANET* TO RULE.

RETURN? ARE YOU *OUT OF YOUR MINDS?*

SCIENCE IS SO *ADVANCED* OUT HERE THAT I MAY BE ABLE TO PUT *ALL* MY THEORIES INTO PRACTICE! OF COURSE, WITH ALL THE *TECHNOLOGY--*

I WILL STAY, TOO. *SVRENSKI* WILL *NEVER* FIND ME HERE.

WHO'S *SVRENSKI*?

SVRENSKI? I DIDN'T SAY "SVRENSKI".

SO, I'M GOING BACK HOME *ALONE*?

NO, MISS SLOAN. *I'M* GOING WITH YOU.

YOU *ARE?*

THERE'S *NOTHING* FOR ME IN MY TIME.

MAYBE IF I GO BACK TO WHERE THE MUTATIONS ALL *STARTED*, I COULD STOP IT FROM EVER *HAPPENING*.

AND THEN MAYBE...

MAYBE WE COULD...

NEXT—
TWIN INFINITY . . .